ASTRONAUT FIRSTS

By S.L. Hamilton

VISIT US AT
WWW.ABDOPUBLISHING.COM

Published by ABDO Publishing Company, 8000 West 78th Street, Suite 310, Edina, MN 55439. Copyright ©2011 by Abdo Consulting Group, Inc. International copyrights reserved in all countries. No part of this book may be reproduced in any form without written permission from the publisher. A&D Xtreme™ is a trademark and logo of ABDO Publishing Company.

Printed in the United States of America, North Mankato, Minnesota.
112010
012011

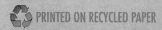 PRINTED ON RECYCLED PAPER

Editor: John Hamilton
Graphic Design: Sue Hamilton
Cover Design: John Hamilton
Cover Photo: NASA
Interior Photos: AP-pg 11; Corbis-pgs 7, 18 & 19; Getty Images-pgs 10 & 11; Granger Collection-pg 16; NASA-pgs 1, 2, 3, 4, 5, 6, 8, 9, 12, 13, 14, 15, 18, 20, 21, 22, 23, 24, 25, 26, 27, 28, 29, 30, 31 & 32; Photo Researchers-pgs 6, 17 & 20.

Library of Congress Cataloging-in-Publication Data

Hamilton, Sue L., 1959-
  Astronaut firsts / S.L. Hamilton.
     p. cm. -- (Xtreme space)
  Includes bibliographical references and index.
  ISBN 978-1-61714-736-4 (alk. paper)
  1. Manned space flight--Chronology--Juvenile literature. 2. Outer space--Exploration--Juvenile literature. 3. Astronauts--Juvenile literature. I. Title.
  TL873.H36 2011
  629.45--dc22
                    2010039862

CONTENTS

Astronaut Robert Crippen was the
first to pilot a reusable spacecraft,
space shuttle *Columbia*, in April 1981.

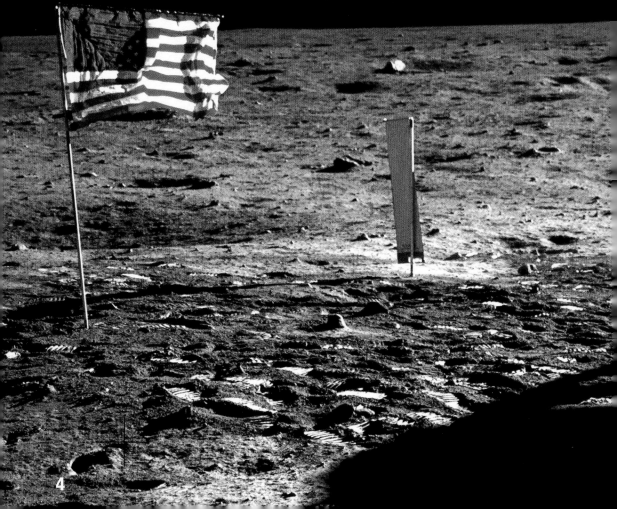

SPACE

For more than 60 years, people have used their courage and knowledge to explore the wonders waiting in space.

FIRSTS

Xtreme Quote

"Here men from the Planet Earth first set foot upon the Moon..."
~Sign placed by Neil Armstrong, July 1969

FIRST ANIMALS

On November 3, 1957, the Russian dog Laika became the first animal to orbit the Earth. She flew aboard *Sputnik 2*.

Sputnik 2

In Space

Malyshka in her space suit in 1957.

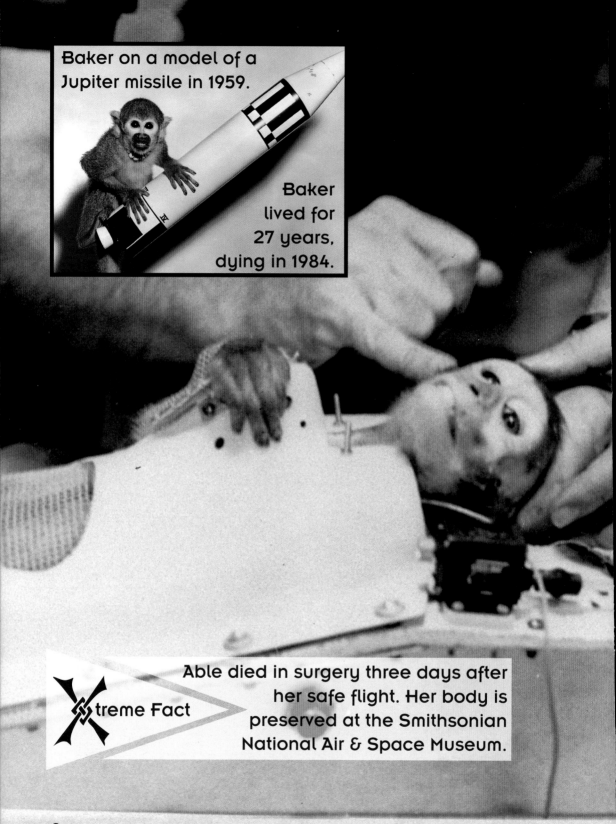

Baker on a model of a Jupiter missile in 1959.

Baker lived for 27 years, dying in 1984.

Able died in surgery three days after her safe flight. Her body is preserved at the Smithsonian National Air & Space Museum.

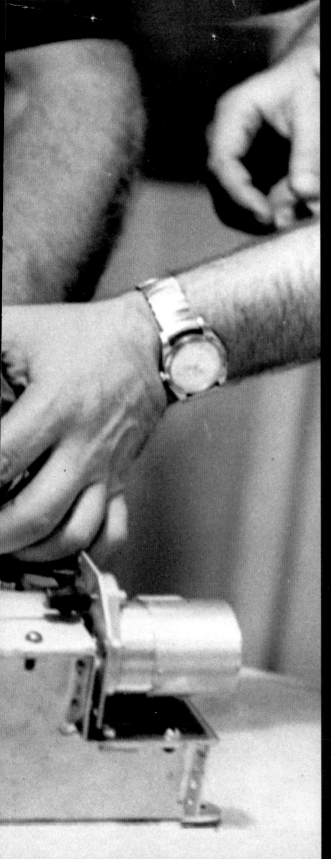

Monkeynauts

On May 28, 1959, Able (a rhesus monkey) and Baker (a squirrel monkey) became the first United States animal astronauts to survive spaceflight. They soared 360 miles (579 km) above Earth's surface in the nose cone of a Jupiter missile. Able and Baker traveled at a top speed of 10,000 mph (16,093 kph) for 16 minutes before returning safely to Earth.

First People

IN SPACE

Cosmonaut Yuri Gagarin was the first human in outer space. He was sent up in the *Vostok 1* spacecraft by the Soviet Union on April 12, 1961. Gagarin spent one hour and 48 minutes in space, before returning safely to Earth to worldwide fame.

Yuri Gagarin was 5' 2" (157 cm) tall. His short height made it easy for him to fit in the small *Vostok 1* cockpit.

First American in Space

Alan Shepard Jr. became the first American to go into space. A Navy test pilot, Shepard became a NASA astronaut in 1959. Millions of people watched him travel into space and return safely on May 5, 1961, aboard the Mercury *Freedom 7* spacecraft.

Xtreme Quote

"Light this candle."

~Alan Shepard, May 5, 1961

FIRST AMERICAN TO

John Glenn Jr.

On February 20, 1962, John Glenn became the first American to orbit the Earth. He saw the sun set and rise from more than 100 miles (161 km) above the Earth.

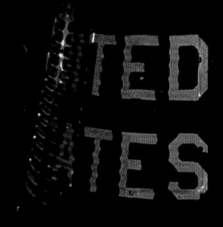

Xtreme Quote

"That sure was a short day."
~John Glenn in orbit

ORBIT THE EARTH

John Glenn enters the *Friendship 7* spacecraft at Cape Canaveral, Florida, for his 4-hour, 55-minute, 23-second mission.

Friendship 7

FIRST WOMEN

Cosmonaut Valentina Tereshkova was launched into space aboard *stok 6* on June 16, 1963. The 26-year-old cosmonaut spent almost three days in space before returning to Earth. This was longer than all American astronauts combined at that time.

In Space

Some of Tereshkova's flight time was broadcast on TV in 1963.

Xtreme Quote

"Anyone who has spent any time in space will love it for the rest of their lives." ~Valentina Tereshkova

First American Woman in Space

Sally Ride
became
the first
American woman in
space. She traveled
as a crew member
of the space shuttle
Challenger on
June 18, 1983. At
the time, she was
also the youngest
American to travel
into space. She was
32 years old.

"I felt very honored, and I knew that people would be watching very closely."   ~Sally Ride

FIRST

Cosmonaut Alexei Leonov took the first walk in space on March 18, 1965. He was outside his *Voskhod 2* spacecraft for about 12 minutes.

SPACEWALKS

On June 3, 1965, astronaut Edward White became the first American to walk in space. White spent 23 minutes outside his *Gemini 4* capsule.

NASA calls a spacewalk an EVA: Extravehicular Activity.

MOON

On July 20, 1969, aboard the lunar module *Eagle*, astronauts Neil Armstrong and Edwin "Buzz" Aldrin Jr. became the first men to land on the Moon.

FIRSTS

With the world watching, *Apollo 11*'s commander, Neil Armstrong, became the first man to walk on the Moon.

First Driver & Vehicle

The first to drive a vehicle on the Moon was *Apollo 15*'s astronaut David Scott. The battery-powered Rover-1 moved across the Moon's surface for the first time on July 31, 1971.

The Lunar Roving Vehicle's maximum speed was clocked at 11 miles per hour (18 kph) by *Apollo 17*'s Eugene Cernan.

Xtreme Quote

The Lunar Roving Vehicle (LRV) was commonly called the "moon buggy."

FIRST AMERICANS TO

Skylab

LIVE IN SPACE

Astronauts Charles "Pete" Conrad, Paul Weitz, and Joseph Kerwin spent 28 days living in space as the first crew of Skylab. They arrived on May 25, 1973.

Eating

Shower

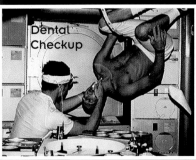
Dental Checkup

Exercise

The first long-term crew of the International Space Station arrived on November 2, 2000. The members of Expedition 1 were American William Shepherd and Russians Yuri Gidzenko and Sergei Krikalev. The three lived and worked at the station until March 18, 2001. They returned to Earth aboard the space shuttle *Discovery*.

Yuri Gidzenko   William Shepherd   Sergei Krikalev

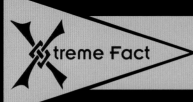

At 803 days, Sergei Krikalev has spent more time in space than any other person so far.

International Space Station in March 2001

THE

Apollo Space Program

An American space exploration program that ran from 1963 to 1972. Run by the National Aeronautics and Space Administration (NASA), the program's goal was to land astronauts on the Moon and return them safely to Earth. The first Moon landing was achieved by *Apollo 11* on July 20, 1969.

International Space Station (ISS)

An Earth-orbiting space station designed by NASA, the European Space Agency, the Russian Federal Space Agency, the Japan Aerospace Exploration Agency, and the Canadian Space Agency, as well as other countries around the world. The ISS allows astronauts and scientists to live and work in space. Construction of the ISS began in orbit in 1998 and is planned to be completed in 2011.

National Aeronautics and Space Administration (NASA)

A U.S. government agency started in 1958. NASA's goals include space exploration, as well as increasing

GLOSSARY

people's understanding of Earth, our solar system, and the universe. One major NASA facility is the John F. Kennedy Space Center in Florida.

Skylab
The first space station launched by the United States. Skylab orbited the Earth from 1973 to 1979. It entered Earth's orbit and broke apart in 1979.

Space Shuttle
America's first reusable space vehicle. NASA developed five different orbiters: *Columbia*, *Challenger*, *Atlantis*, *Discovery*, and *Endeavour*. Two shuttles and their crews were destroyed in accidents: *Challenger* in 1986 and *Columbia* in 2003.

Test Pilot
A person who flies new or experimental aircraft to test the machine's flight worthiness.

INDEX

Cosmonaut Valeri Polyakov has the record for the longest stay in space: 437 days.